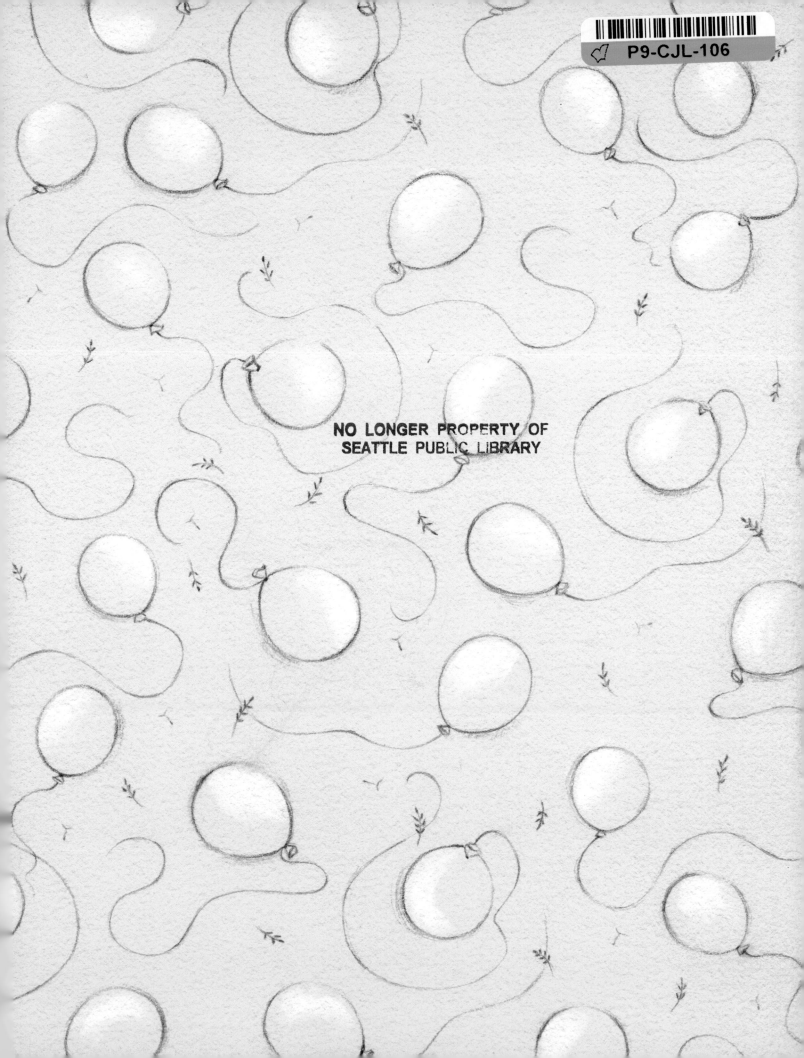

To Bundo and to first friends everywhere —G.M.

For my Mum and Dad for always supporting and encouraging me. With love —G.F.

THIS IS A BORZOI BOOK PUBLISHED BY ALFRED A. KNOPF

Text copyright © 2019 by Gretchen McLellan

Jacket art and interior illustrations copyright © 2019 by Gillian Flint

All rights reserved. Published in the United States by Alfred A. Knopf, an imprint of Random House Children's Books, a division of Penguin Random House LLC, New York. Knopf, Borzoi Books, and the colophon are registered trademarks of Penguin Random House LLC.

Visit us on the Web! rhcbooks.com

Educators and librarians, for a variety of teaching tools, visit us at RHTeachersLibrarians.com

Library of Congress Cataloging-in-Publication Data is available upon request.
ISBN 978-1-5247-6668-9 (trade) — ISBN 978-1-5247-6669-6 (lib. bdg.) —
ISBN 978-1-5247-6670-2 (ebook)

The illustrations in this book were created using watercolors, pastels, and pencil.
The text of this book is set in 20-point Beton Com Light.

MANUFACTURED IN CHINA
February 2019
10 9 8 7 6 5 4 3 2 1

First Edition

Button
and
Bundle

By Gretchen McLellan

Illustrated by Gillian Flint

ALFRED A. KNOPF

New York

Button and Bundle were friends. First friends.

Their dolls were, too.

It was always Button and Bundle,

Petal and Rose.

Weaving daisy chains,
blowing wishes,
and singing their song.

Button and Bundle made clothes and furniture
and a house for Petal and Rose.

They pretended they were small enough to
fit inside and promised to live there forever.

But one day, everything changed.
Button had to move away.

They had a good-bye party,
but there was nothing good about good-bye.

There was nothing good about
their together-story ending.
Button and Bundle hid and
held each other tight.

When it was time to go,
Button, still warm from Bundle's last hug,
told Petal to be brave.

But Button didn't think they'd ever be happy again.

In their new house, Petal wanted to stay in her bed.
Button asked if she wanted to come out and play,
but Petal never did.

It was a lonely, blue time for Button and Petal.

One day, a balloon as yellow as the sun arrived
with a song in the breeze.
And Button knew what she needed to do.

She tied a basket to the balloon and nestled Petal
inside. "Find Bundle and Rose," she said.

On the top of a big green hill, Button kissed
Petal good-bye and let the balloon go.
As the balloon rose, Button's heart rose, too.

She dreamed of Petal on her journey and of the celebration when Petal touched down.

Bundle would decorate the dollhouse with ribbons and buttercups.

There would be tiny cakes and lemonade.

And Button danced in the yellow sun,
imagining Bundle and Rose and Petal
together again.

Wearing crowns in their hair,
whispering wishes,
and singing their song.
Button sang it, too.

One day, while she was looking for fairies in the garden,
a face peeked at her through the fence.
It was a girl and a horse with wings.

She was looking for fairies, too.
And friends.

Leah gave Button a unicorn named Sparkles.

Soon it was Button and Leah, Sparkles and Crystal.

Wearing feathers and wings,

sharing secrets,

and singing a new song.

Button and Bundle's song wove through it like ribbons.

And when Button sang with all her heart,
the song carried through the sky like the
yellow balloon.

And she knew that Bundle and Rose
and Petal heard it, too.

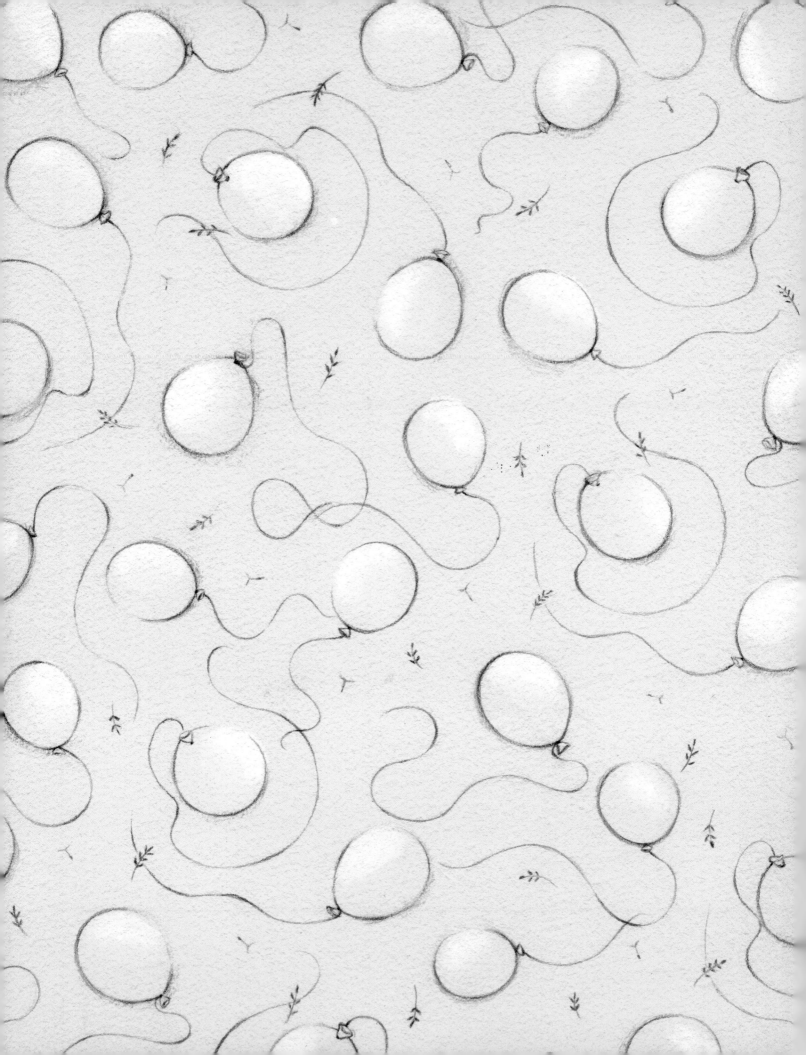